Dead Lay

Tales of Zombie Erotica

Alisha Adkins

Other Works by the Author

Flesh Eaters

Making the Best of the Zombie Apocalypse

Zombie Gras

Daydreams of Seppuku

Twisted Tales for Twisted Minds

Shadow Schism

Dedication

For Jackie.

Contents

The Help

Reclusive by nature, Lydia had lived a quiet, solitary life before the zombie apocalypse. She worked from home and, with the assistance of the Internet, was able to have no more than passing interactions with other human beings.

Lydia had accepted this isolation -- hell, she had practically embraced it, convincing herself that human interactions were too complicated anyway.

"Social connections come with expectations and obligations. Obligations which enslave us," she told herself. She knew that, for most people, such ties enriched their lives. But weren't bonds that anchor and enrich human lives still fetters nonetheless? Most people preferred not to acknowledge their constrictive properties, but in Lydia's eyes, they were still chains.

So what was the alternative? Complete isolation? Choosing a life free of human contact over one with obligations?"

She had thought so. It was a lonely option, one that did not come without cost. But the zombie apocalypse had offered her an alternative.

Since the apocalypse, companionship had become much simpler to obtain. Life, or the living dead, if one were to get technical about it, came fairly cheaply in this brave new world.

The "apocalypse" hadn't been as bad as it had sounded. Sure, the initial outbreak had been chaotic, but it was quickly brought under control. Soon enough, the undead had become just another commodity to be bought and sold.

Yes, the undead were dangerous, but when properly handled, they made excellent slaves, although that was an extremely politically incorrect, inflammatory term for the services they rendered, of course. In the common vernacular, the preferred term was simply "the help." The help were incomparable workers as long as the work was simple enough labor for them to accomplish -- permanently indentured workers that never needed to rest and were incapable of unionizing. Forty hour work weeks did not apply. No breaks necessary.

And they made very obliging domestic servants as well, although again, your demands had to be relatively simple.

It wasn't like one was really opening one's home to a rotting ghoul, per se. That would have been barbaric. No, purchased help was always sold enhanced. The teeth had been removed, of course -- that feature was always included. The help that Lydia purchased had also been injected with preservatives to slow the rate of decay; that was another baseline feature. And, although she hadn't splurged on the luxury package, she had taken the standard options -- which included essential oil immersion, an odor-reduction process in which the zombie's skin was infused with the client's choice of scented oil (which could be chosen from a large standard catalog selection or, for a nominal fee, customized to order). She had considered lilac or cinnamon, but settled upon the scent of cedar. It wasn't her favorite smell, but she had heard that it lasted longer than others and was one of the most effective at masking the smell of decay.

The transition wasn't instantaneous, but soon enough, it stopped snapping its jaws at her and resigned itself to its fate.

They got used to one another. In fact, as Lydia grew accustomed to seeing it every day, she began to find her zombie almost cute in a "so ugly it's cute" pug dog sort of way.

Zombies could be trained to perform a variety of basic household tasks, although dish washing was not recommended. It was unsanitary to eat from dishes handled by a zombie, and prolonged submersion of a zombie's hands in water had nasty consequences. Other housework though, such as cleaning and laundry, were learned without much incident. But none of these tasks were the true purpose for which Lydia had purchased her zombie, and it was its true purpose at which it would really shine.

When Lydia had been a younger woman, she had been able to stifle her libido with ease. But every passing year seemed to make quashing it more impossible. Desire, like bile she could not keep down, bubbled up uncontrollably from her depths. Hormonal

12

changes had made her lecherous. She had become every lascivious man that she had ever hated, unable to stop herself from wantonly objectifying men as nothing more than useful meat. She hated observing this trait in herself, but she was powerless to control it. It seemed to Lydia that post-thirty hormones twisted women into impotent predators -- cruel birds of prey that held back only due to a lack of confidence created by aging bodies and fading beauty of which they were so acutely aware. Women like her hunted in vain, never leaving the shadows, tracking their quarry but never pouncing, all the while yearning to swoop down on the men they watched and strip them to their bones.

The complex nature of human relationships required too much; it was too difficult. But as the mistress of an undead servant, such concerns were unnecessary. In fact, zombies were less trouble than even a pet since you wouldn't kill them if you neglected their care. You could forget to feed one and leave it in a dusty corner for a year or more, and it would still be there, milling about and bumping into things, when you next remembered that it was there. At worst, it would

13

have lost a limb or two to decay, and these days a multitude of businesses offered cybernetic tune-ups at competitive prices.

There were fringe groups that lobbied against zombie servitude, of course. They argued that zombie enslavement was a question of morality. The relevant issues revolved around whether or not a zombie was a sentient being. Essentially, the debate seemed akin to the issue of animal cruelty. Surely zombies were no more sentient than a horse harnessed to a plough or a hamster that ran in a wheel. So did they feel pain? Could they suffer? Lydia could see that her zombie certainly took no pleasure in its tasks, but she did not think it looked unduly unhappy. In fact, it was essentially expressionless. Lydia knew that animals expressed happiness, sadness, fear, and pain, but it seemed that zombies did not. Maybe they were no more sentient than furniture -- chairs to be moved from place to place.

Not that it mattered. Lydia did not concern herself with pointless moral debates. Her zombie was her property, and it made her life easier. She had lacked

14

companionship; now there was another presence stumbling about the rooms of her house. She had had housework; now she had only leisure time at her disposal. She had been sexually frustrated; now she had release.

The zombie's sexual obligations to its mistress were its true purpose, the reason she had spent all that money on it. It was the ultimate sex toy.

She named him Heracles. Sexually, his only drawback was that he always had to wear a condom; it was the only way she could avoid bacterial infections. But this minor detraction from intercourse was more than made up for by his natural affinity for cunnilingus. Perhaps it was facilitated by his lack of teeth, or maybe it was just because he wanted to eat her flesh, but the things he did with his tongue made her positively writhe and squeal in ecstasy. She didn't even notice the dental dam.

Heracles was a surprisingly smart and talented zombie. He learned so quickly how to unroll the condom to sheath himself! And in no time he had picked up on and begun proficiently mimicking her desired rhythm.   Lydia found herself beaming with pride when she watched him.

Lydia affectionately patted her meat puppet on his head whenever she passed him cleaning in the house. And, when the urge struck, as it did two or three times a day, she would pull him to her, squeezing coagulated blood into his penis with her hand, and order him to fuck her.

"Heracles, come here! Heracles, fuck me!" she demanded.

Expressionless, Heracles dutifully produced a condom from the pouch of his apron and obeyed.

The Carrier

Heracles drew himself out slowly, just as his mistress had taught him, lingering at the opening, and then thrust forcefully, burying his organ deep as the woman moaned and shuddered beneath him.

As he moved in and out of her, the friction caused putrefied layers of skin to slough away from his penis and mix with her bodily fluids, acting like goopy Astroglide.

He bent his head down and ran his slimy black tongue over her erect nipples; she shuddered with pleasure.

Lydia's cheeks flushed with rage when she saw them.

"What the hell do you think you're doing?" she cried, dropping her groceries.

In her own bed! She had found Heracles, her zombie house servant, and Marsha, her brother's wife, together in her own bed!

When she had told her sister-in-law that she could stop by to pick up her tuna casserole recipe, she had never imagined this.

Marsha tried to wave Lydia away with one hand while the other still clutched tightly to the zombie's withered arm, but Lydia ran to the bed and forcibly pulled them apart. Lydia yanked Heracles off of her sister-in-law; the startled zombie tumbled indelicately to the floor like a sack of old potatoes.

"You could have at least let me finish!" Marsha said indignantly as she smoothed down her mussed hair and began to gather up her scattered clothes.

Lydia huffed and spluttered, too angry to get out words.

"Wait, are you actually mad?" Marsha asked, furrowing her brow in amused consternation.

"You have a real relationship -- you don't *need* a surrogate companion!" Lydia finally spat.

"*Surrogate*? He's just an animated sex toy."

"He's *mine*!" Lydia shrieked.

As the women spoke, Heracles, unnoticed, clumsily picked himself up from the floor and stumbled into the nearest corner.

"Why are you so angry, Lydia?" Marsha asked, genuinely puzzled. And then it dawned on her. "Oh, my God, you're jealous!" she exclaimed.

"But how can you be jealous? That's completely irrational. It's an organic appliance. It was just performing its job." Marsha said, buttoning her blouse. "It's not a lover. It's just a *zombie*. It's like me using your toaster. "

Flustered, Lydia retorted, "Well, he's still my property! You should ask before you use him. I wouldn't come over to your house and use your vacuum cleaner without asking you first -- let alone get off with it! And what about my brother... your husband?"

"Oh, please. It's hardly cheating. If this is cheating," she said, with a dismissive gesture toward the naked grey animated corpse standing awkwardly in the corner, "then so is getting off with my vibrator."

After Lydia had forcibly ejected her sister-in-law from her home, she was left to ponder her own tumultuous emotions. Why did she feel this way? She couldn't explain it, let alone justify it.

*****

Marsha initially didn't give any thought to the fact that she had not used protection. It wasn't like a zombie could get her pregnant.

However, when she went to pee after having decidedly less satisfying sex with her husband later that evening, she grew alarmed when foul smelling chunks of fleshy goop began to fall out of her vagina, splashing as they plopped into the toilet.

"Oh, shit," Marsha said under her breath, frantically wiping herself.

Dropping to her knees, she began to sift through the fleshy debris in the toilet with her hands. As she lifted the slimy pieces out to better examine them, their smell made her gag. Terrified, she wondered if these handfuls of stringy, gelatinous tissue that oozed from between her fingers were actually pieces of her vagina.

*****

Marsha lay awake all night, listening to the sound of her husband's snoring. By the next morning, she was running a slight fever and her skin felt oddly fizzy.

Overcome with worry that she was developing some sort of massive infection, Marsha waited impatiently for her husband to leave for work. As soon as he was finally out of the door, Marsha ran to the bedroom and tore off her clothes. She hurriedly sprawled out on the carpet, laying naked in front of the full length mirror and spreading her legs. It was difficult to stay in a position that kept her pussy open wide while also getting her head close enough to really examine the area. She teetered as she peered, scrutinizing her genitals.

Her labia seemed a bit more purple than she remembered, but she had never examined herself like this before, so it was hard to really tell. Were her lips slightly puffy? She wasn't sure. As far as she could tell, her vagina still looked fairly normal. Could all of those fleshy pieces that fell out of her have just been parts of Lydia's zombie?

As soon as her doctor's office opened, she made an appointment. Unfortunately, the earliest appointment available wasn't until the following week. *I'll probably be dead by then*, she thought.

*****

However, as days past, in spite of her anxiety and sleeplessness, Marsha began to feel better and better. By the time the day of her appointment arrived, she was so sure that she was alright that she almost skipped it.

"I had unprotected sex with my sister-in-law's zombie, and some stuff came out of me later that day," Marsha explained to the doctor. "Since then, I've felt fine though," she added quickly. "I think I just panicked. I really don't think anything is wrong with me," she said dismissively, hoping that the doctor would readily agree.

"Unprotected sex with a zombie can have dire consequences, Mrs. Grote. You do appear to be healthy, but I'll order a blood test so that we can be sure," Dr. Duerkenpeak said.

The nurse drew some blood, and then Marsha returned home.

*****

Marsha returned to her daily routine, and everything seemed perfectly normal. Well, almost everything. Herbert, her husband, seemed to have inexplicably adopted a new air of complacency.

"Would it be alright if I took the car tomorrow?" Marsha asked.

"Yes, dear," Herbert grunted.

Herbert was typically very possessive about his convertible, and Marsha had fully expected him to tell her no. Since he was being uncharacteristically agreeable, she decided to push it.

"Huh. Okay, thanks. Well, how about if I..."

"Yes, dear."

Marsha raised an eyebrow suspiciously.

"Well then," she said, hunting for the most outlandish request she muster, "I was thinking that I'd withdraw your 401k and use it to have a complete plastic surgery makeover. I know you were planning to use it to live in comfort after you retired, but this would be much better for my self-esteem."

"Yes, dear."

His voice did not change even a half octave. It was utterly flat, monotone, without a hint of concern.

Puzzled, Marsha's mouth began to flap as she tried to find an appropriate response, but then the phone rang.

"Hello?"

"Mrs. Grote?" a man asked.

"Yes, this is she," she said distractedly, still staring at her husband.

"This is Dr. Duerkenpeak. We received the results of your blood work. I'm afraid that your blood test came back positive for STZ."

"STZ?" she asked, confused.

"Yes, Sexually Transmitted Zombiism. But, of course, since you are not displaying any external signs of zombiism, it is likely that you are just a carrier. Just be sure to always use protection with your sexual partner, as you could infect them."

"Oh. I see," Marsha said slowly. "Well, thank you."

She hung up the phone.

Herbert didn't ask who had called. In fact, he gave no indication that he was even aware that there had been a phone call.

"Herbert, come here," Marsha ordered.

Dutifully, he shuffled over to her.

Looking closely at her husband for the first time in years, Marsha noticed an unnatural pallor to his skin. His face was actually almost grey, and patches of skin appeared to be flaking away from his cheeks.

"Herbert, you haven't developed some kind of eczema, have you?" Marsha inquired.

"Mmmpphhhffft," Herbert replied.

Marsha slowly nodded.

"Herbert, eat my pussy," she demanded, hiking up her skirt.

Obediently, Herbert dropped to his knees, pulled her underwear aside, and submerged his face in her. He licked Marsha's folds, lapped at her clit, and then thrust his tongue inside of her.

Although still a bit dismayed, Marsha squirmed happily.

*****

The following morning, Herbert got up and went to work just as he always did, even though he had not slept during the night. It seemed that he no longer required sleep. He had just lain in bed and stared blankly up at the ceiling with glassy eyes for eight hours. *No more snoring!* Marsha marveled.

Marsha felt a growing affection for Herbert now, in his new state. While he was getting ready for work, she couldn't resist stopping him to tenderly straighten his tie and gently advise him, "put on more cologne, dear."

After he left, she hurried out to meet a friend for breakfast. She was bursting to tell someone about Herbert's transformation.

Joining her friend Margaret at Cafeing Cafe, she ordered a croissant and then launched into her exciting news.

"This is the best thing that's ever happened to me!" she spouted.

Margaret was unconvinced. "If he's a zombie, isn't he rotting? I mean, that doesn't really sound very good."

"Oh, I suppose his skin *is* a little rotten in places, but he really doesn't look that bad, considering. The real transformation is in his demeanor."

"But what about work? Herbert makes a six-figure salary. If he can't perform his job..."

Marsha beamed. "He still gets up and goes to work without complaint. Nobody seems to have noticed there. After all, he's an executive; he probably hasn't really done anything at the office in years. Truth be told," she added, lowering her voice, "I think his co-workers are probably happier now with this new, less verbose, version of Herbert."

Marsha's friend shook her head.

"Margaret, I'm telling you, in the bedroom, he is now my passive, capitulating sex servant! Anything I want, I get. It's a dream come true. You know how I used to have to cajole Herbert into sex? Well, now he services me at my command – I get it when I want it, how I want it! Besides," Marsha added wistfully, "I think he's kind of sweet this way."

"Really?" Margaret said, suddenly beginning to look interested. "You know, I think I might have an idea."

*****

Death tended to emasculate men, rendering them far less threatening. Sure, zombies wanted to eat the flesh of the living, but the removal of teeth proved to be a simple fix. Taking the teeth out of a real human relationship was a far more tricky procedure.

Underneath, it seemed that Marsha and all of her female friends secretly harbored a sexually predatory nature. They were all cougars, lurking in the shadows, waiting for the opportunity to pounce. Once word got out, women Marsha hadn't spoken to in years started calling out of the blue. Soon, strangers began calling as well.

Zombie husbands didn't argue or make demands, and for a certain type of woman, this was ideal. So it was always the same. Although initially the caller feigned horror over Herbert's condition, she would soon admit her jealousy. Then she would finally reveal the real reason that she had called: could Marsha help her? If Marsha would be willing to fuck her husband, she would be more than happy to arrange everything. Typically, this was easily done; the wife need only pretend that she was finally agreeing to her husband's long-held sexual fantasy of bringing in a new partner.

Marsha began renting herself out to them. She fucked their husbands, infecting them so that they too would become accommodating, willing sex slaves. Although her fee was high, she actually usually enjoyed the work.

In truth, being a carrier was a blessing. Marsha embarked with gusto upon her new (and highly lucrative) career as a courtesan for hire, having sex with

29

the husbands of voracious housewives. After all, she was providing a community service.

The Equipment

Her heart was pounding, and it was difficult to breathe. A sense of panic had begun to rise in Lydia's body. Though the sensation originated in her chest, it quickly swelled, overflowing and radiating outwards, hot and tingly, flooding her extremities with adrenaline.

Things had been going so well. Lydia had been indulging in her mid-morning fuck with Heracles, her zombie servant. He had pounded her hard, just as she liked it, and she had cum with a satisfying shudder. However, when she waved him away to resume his cleaning duties, he drew back, but his member didn't.

At first she hadn't understood what had happened. Heracles matter-of-factly pulled up his pants and shambled off to retrieve a feather duster, but she still felt him inside of her. She lay there in a post-orgasm stupor for several minutes before giving it much thought.

Then Lydia lazily drew a hand between her legs to cup her vagina, which was still gently buzzing with pleasure, and the panic took hold.

Shreds of slimy flesh were hanging out of her. As she frantically felt around down there, what had happened became horribly clear. Heracles had broken off inside of her. His cock was still in there.

What was she going to do? She lay there, trying not to hyperventilate, obsessively touching the strips of spongy meat that hung from between her vaginal lips. She tried to pull the penis out, but she just couldn't get a good grip. Although the base of his shaft partially protruded from her, it was so slimy that it was difficult to grasp and, whenever she did get a hold of a piece, it tore as soon as she tried to pull it.

She was terrified. Was she going to wind up infected? Heracles had worn a condom, as he always did, but this unexpected mishap was putting her in contact with at least bits of his bare flesh. Would she become a zombie? Or die of a massive bacterial infection? Maybe her vagina would become necrotic. At the very least, she was going to wind up with toxic shock if she didn't get this hunk of rotten meat out of her.

Finally, she took a deep breath, tried to still her heart enough that it might not explode, and dialed 911.

"...its penis came loose. Yes, that's right, "Lydia said, speaking as clearly as she could into the phone. She covered her eyes with her free hand as if to shield herself from her own embarrassment.

"Yes, it broke off... inside of me. Yes," she said, nodding into the receiver.

"No, I tried that. I can't get it out," she said, choking back a frustrated sob.

*****

After a hazmat removal team had extracted the member from her, sterilized the area, and then left, Lydia initially just wanted to bury her head in shame. You haven't truly known embarrassment until a man in a hazmat suit extracts a rotten penis from your vagina with forceps.

However, after a few days of wallowing, Lydia's libido again began to rear its head. At first it was a periodic, fluttering whim that she resolutely ignored. Then it became a persistent, nagging itch that she solemnly denied. But finally, it returned to its full

33

strength, a raging current of need to which she could only succumb.

Unfortunately, Lydia's tool of choice was no longer available. The hazmat team had sealed it away securely in a jar and taken it with them.

There was no way around it. It was time to take Heracles in for repairs.

*****

"This happens with all male zombies eventually," Doctor Schock mumbled to himself as he examined Heracles.

"Yes, yes, just as one would expect: natural rate of decomposition, a few minor areas of liquefaction, and some patches of pesky insect larvae. I'll prescribe a pesticide lotion that will clear that right up," he said.

Lydia did not share Dr. Schock's lack of concern. "But what about his... member?" she asked, her voice lined with a sharp edge of desperation.

"Hmmph. Nothing to worry about at all," the doctor declared, gesturing for Lydia to take a seat next to his desk. Heracles remained motionless, perched atop the examination table, his vacant eyes staring forward, unblinking. His naked grey body looked unnaturally small and vulnerable under the room's harsh fluorescent lights.

"As I said, this happens with all male zombies eventually. Appendages are bound to break off over time... especially if the appendages are being put to regular use," he added, clearing his throat.

"The good news though is that now Heracles can have a detachable penis. The technology has really advanced in the past few years, so there are a wide variety of options available," the doctor said brightly with an encouraging smile. "Today's prosthetics are extremely life-like -- or maybe I should say undead-like," he chuckled.

Lydia said nothing, so he continued. "Yes, well, ahem, anyway, Heracles can be fitted with a fully functional cybernetic penis. These come with a life-time warranty - your life-time, not his," he added jovially. This time the doctor managed to swallow the urge to chuckle at his own quip, although he still couldn't resist indulging in a faint smirk.

Lydia's expression did not change. For her, this was no laughing matter. Heracles's equipment was serious business.

"You could even go with a collection of interchangeable prosthetics," Dr. Schock suggested. "They come in a full range of sizes for whatever mood may strike you, as it were."

*****

Heracles had been "in the shop" for nearly a week, and Lydia was positively beside herself by the time the day of his homecoming finally arrived.

When the orderlies delivered Heracles, they walked him up Lydia's driveway at the end of a catch pole. He was bound and muzzled, which seemed excessive to Lydia since her zombie had no teeth.

Once unfettered inside her house, Heracles returned to his housekeeping duties as if he had never left. Lydia, however, watched him with concern. He moved listlessly, which was normal for him, but she thought his motions seemed more telegraphed -- slower, more erratic, and somewhat jerky, almost like those of someone in pain. Maybe it was just her imagination.

Although she genuinely tried to exercise restraint, Lydia was able to wait little more than an hour before she broke down and called Heracles to her.

The zombie came when it was called, immediately lumbering toward the sound of her voice. Seeing Lydia lying on the bed with her legs spread apart, Heracles understood what Lydia clearly wanted and dutifully began to rummage in the pocket of his apron, retrieving one of his five interchangeable penises.

At the clinic, technicians had fitted Heracles with a socket, drilled deep into his pelvis, to ensure that a wide variety of prosthetic devices would readily snap in and remain well anchored.

Snapping a mid-size model into the socket, Heracles approached his mistress.

Lydia gestured at him to get down on his knees and then, grasping the wispy scraps of hair that remained on his head, she buried his face in her. She writhed in pleasure as the zombie slurped loudly.

Soon desperately wet with anticipation, she could wait no longer to have a cock inside of her. She slipped Heracles's prosthetic organ between her folds and immediately let out an involuntary moan. He was bigger and harder than before, filling her up.

"Pump me," she directed him in a lustful snarl. Expressionless, the zombie obeyed.

Thrusting in the rhythm she had taught him, progressively faster and harder, Heracles quickly brought Lydia to orgasm. She came with a shriek of sheer ecstasy.

After, panting, she waved the zombie away to resume his housework. Then, relaxed and blissfully sated, she lay in bed, still letting aftershocks of pleasure wash over her.

However, even in the peaceful calm of post-coitus euphoria, in the far corner of her mind, a thought was troubling Lydia. Ever since Heracles had lost his cock, Lydia simply couldn't dispel the notion that her zombie had a finite number of uses -- a definite expiration date that he would reach at some point in the future.

The realization saddened her.

She asked herself, what would she do when Heracles's tongue rotted away, as it was bound to do? There were no reputable tongue prosthetic manufacturers, so she knew that she would eventually be forced to replace him.

Lydia had come to rely upon Heracles so much over the past two years that she had owned him. He was her most treasured appliance, a valuable piece of household equipment. When he wore out, she would have to train a new zombie, and there was no guarantee that his replacement would ever be able to match his skill.

Lydia sighed wistfully in sad resignation of her inevitable future loss.

Step-Daughter of the Damned

Lydia was having Heracles try out the new micro-penis attachment she had purchased specifically for anal sex when the door bell rang.

She ignored it at first, trying to stay in the moment.

"Fuck me in the ass! Plough me!" she coaxed, holding onto the fantasy that she was taking a much bigger cock than the short, slender prosthetic that was really snapped into her zombie's groin.

The door bell rang again with the extended buzz of an impatient caller.

"Damn it," Lydia sighed, getting up and throwing on a robe.

*****

Opening the door, Lydia found an attractive young woman with a sour expression waiting for her.

"I've come to put my father to rest," the woman said.

"Excuse me?" Lydia replied, frowning.

"I've come for my father."

Lydia blinked at the woman, uncomprehending. "I'm sorry, but you have the wrong house," she said and began to shut the door, but the girl thrust her foot into the doorframe.

"I don't have the wrong house," the young woman said icily.

Sighing, Lydia spoke slowly in the hope that the girl might understand in spite of whatever was wrong with her. "Your... father... is... not... here. You... have... the... wrong... house."

The girl's voice broke, as if something inside of her was tearing, as she said resolutely, "I've come to set my father free, to grant him the peace of eternal sleep."

Growing irritated, Lydia drew herself up to her full height as she said, "Your father isn't here. I don't know what's wrong with you, but it isn't my problem. You need to leave."

"Father!" the woman exclaimed, lunging forward as she spotted Heracles, who was returning to dusting in the foyer. Lydia spread herself across the entryway, just managing to block the woman from entering.

"*That,*" the woman shouted, pointing at Lydia's zombie, "is my father!"

Well, this is a pain in the ass, Lydia thought.

"Dad, Dad!" the girl shouted. Heracles remained engrossed in his household duties; he did not raise his head or show any sign of acknowledgement.

Now in an extreme state of agitation, the woman began screaming, "I am Daisy Marchant, and that is my father! I have rights! You can't keep him a slave here! I *will* put down my father's corpse, so that he can rest in dignity. I have a legal right to his body. Besides, what's wrong with you that you want a corpse in your house, let alone in your bed?"

Neighbors were beginning to peek out of their doorways to see what all the screaming was about.

"Could you please lower your voice?" Lydia snarled as she tried to loosen the girl's grip on her doorframe.

Heracles's daughter continued, shouting "Are you so hard up that you want to fuck a broken down sack of bones?"

"How dare you!" Lydia countered angrily. "I keep him in top physical condition."

She glowered at the girl. "Besides," she said crossly, "why should I even believe you are his daughter? How *can* you be his daughter? You look about twenty-five years old. And my zombie is maybe thirty-five."

"He died ten years ago," the girl said bitterly.

"Even if that were true, that doesn't mean he is any concern of yours." Lydia said, finally managing to push the girl out of the doorway.

"Oh, he is my concern!" the girl exclaimed. "Ma'am, to be blunt, I don't want my father's dick in your dried up old cooch! He no longer has any will of his own. You're raping the dead."

Lydia lost her patience. "Honey, your father's dick fell off almost a year ago. I paid good money for his current equipment. It's my property, not yours."

"I have paperwork. The law grants me dominion over the remains of my father!" the young woman insisted, beginning to rummage in her purse, presumably for documents.

"Well, I have paperwork too. I have a notarized title *and* an extended warranty. So you can take it up with the company!" Lydia shouted back as she slammed the door.

*****

He thrust deeply and a long, extended moan of pleasure escaped from Lydia's lips.

He moaned too, but that was normal for him.

"Faster! Right there!" she hissed.

Obediently, Heracles increased his pace, pounding her in just the right spot until she came explosively.

She gasped in ecstasy and then lay back, panting.

Heracles drew out of her and then gingerly pulled the large-girth penis attachment out of his organic socket. Then he began to ease off of Lydia's body, but suddenly he clumsily fell to one side, toppling off of the bed.

"What the?" Lydia exclaimed, propping herself up on her elbows.

Then she saw the dismembered limb. Heracles had apparently lost his balance because his left arm had broken off. It lay, twitching, next to her hip, rotten flesh and tendons dangling where it had once been attached to his shoulder.

Lydia sighed. She was going to have to get her zombie repaired again. All these service visits were growing tedious, and she wondered if he was going to eventually become composed entirely of prostheses. Thank God she had at least gotten the extended warranty.

On the floor, Heracles was slowly turning in circles as he feebly tried to pick himself up using his remaining arm. He looked like a turtle on its back, spinning hopelessly, legs flailing, as it tried to right itself.

"Alright, hold on," Lydia grumbled at him. She helped her wobbly zombie up and sent him off to resume his housework.

Then it hit her. The Tupperware party! What was she going to do? Having Heracles serve mimosas in this condition was a recipe for disaster.

The doorbell rang.

*****

Lydia looked through the peephole. It was her again – Daisy, the step-daughter of the damned, back again to make trouble. It seemed that she was intent upon visiting every day until she got what she wanted.

"I'm not leaving without my father!" the girl shouted through the door.

Lydia sighed. "Alright, fine, why don't you come in then, instead of making all that racket out there. We can talk about it in here."

She opened the door, and the girl propelled herself inside, looking around frantically for her father.

"He's upstairs. I'll get him in a minute. Just go into the kitchen and sit down. Have some iced tea. It will take me a little while to get him ready. He has a lot of accessories to pack."

Lydia trotted up the stairs.

*****

Lydia had been part of a contingent of women in their forties and fifties who were filled with desires but impotent to fulfill them. Younger men shrank from her, and men her own age lacked the libido to sate her.

Acquiring a zombie house servant had proven to be the perfect solution. There had been bumps along the way, of course. Parts of Heracles dropped off from time to time (seemingly with ever increasing frequency), and she felt the need to keep a suspicious eye trained upon her female acquaintances at all times because she was sure that they all coveted her zombie (or at least the valuable services he rendered so effectively). But these

48

were minor issues. Lydia wouldn't trade Heracles for anything in the world. And *nobody* was going to waltz in and take him away from her.

Whistling cheerfully as she returned from upstairs, Lydia slipped into the kitchen and pierced the girl's arm with the syringe before Heracles' daughter even realized what was happening.

Alarmed, the girl cried, "What are you doing?"

"Nothing to worry about," Lydia tut-tutted. "Just a bit of dear old Dad. You wanted to be closer, didn't you?"

The necrotic material, which Lydia had drawn from the most gangrenous areas of Heracles' dismembered limb, hit the young woman's blood stream almost instantly, and she immediately began to feel woozy. She slipped from the chair.

"Like father, like daughter," Lydia cooed, leaning over her. The girl watched the edges of Lydia's face grow indistinct as she smiled and smoothed her hair.

Once the young woman had lost consciousness, Lydia knocked out her teeth with a few swift swings of a hammer. Viola! Now she had a nice, fresh zombie to do the serving at her Tupperware party.

It was about time she expanded her household staff anyway. Heracles wasn't as efficient as he used to be and really had too many duties for one decomposing zombie. Yes, having an extra zombie around was going to solve all of Lydia's problems.

"I can always use a maid," Lydia reasoned aloud as the girl began to reanimate. "Besides," she said to her new zombie, smiling wickedly, "you're going to be eating a whole lot of my dried up old cooch."

"Now, let me get you an apron."

Pushing Up Daisy

The maid hadn't worked out. It was so hard to find good help these days.

Daisy, Lydia's belligerent step-daughter turned zombie maid, had decomposed at an alarming rate, perhaps because Lydia had not had the proper materials with which to treat her body. Since she had no ownership title for Daisy, she had been forced to simply behead and dismember her and then bury her pieces in the flower bed.

It was a messy problem, but easily solved. Well, except that after a heavy rain, the occasional putrid twitching limb would peek up out of the soil, necessitating reburial. She always sent Heracles out for this task, reasoning that it was as close as he would ever again come to a family reunion.

The experience had soured Lydia on the notion of adding any future staff. It seemed that zombies were a mixed bag; she'd clearly gotten lucky with Heracles. He was special, and there was no guarantee that she'd find another zombie as skilled as he even if she were to add a hundred more to her household. So she had resolved to not take on any more zombies, whether homemade or purchased; she and Heracles were better as a pair -- a single unit.

Sure, he was getting old, but he was tried and true. So what if things dropped off of him now and then? Cybernetic repairs were always available, and he was adept at finding new and inventive ways to please her with him. For instance, he had found a way to wiggle his cybernetic fingers inside of her that absolutely turned her into an orgasmic pile of mush. Really - she couldn't even move for half an hour after he brought her to orgasm that way; she just lay there like jelly, shuddering and letting out little moans into her pillow.

So Lydia resumed her secluded life with Heracles, finding no need to pay much attention to the goings-on of the world outside of her home. However, in the world outside, the tide of public opinion was turning. Zombies, once viewed as useful additions to any household, soon were transformed into pariah after a couple of unfortunate (and particularly gruesome) incidents involving zombified husbands received a disproportionately large amount of media attention. Videos of renegade zombies quickly followed, cropping up on YouTube in droves, and soon, swept up in the panic, half the neighborhood had put their zombies out with the trash.

Noticing the phenomenon on trash days, Lydia began to read a little bit of the anti-zombie propaganda that was suddenly so prolific on the web, but she initially wasn't remotely worried. The media-created frenzy was clearly hogwash. Commercially sold zombies didn't "go rogue." Sure, even she had seen Zombies Gone Bad, the popular reality show, but it was sensationalist tripe. Their footage was invariably of poorly maintained homemade zombies - not quality undead help. You can't expect a cheaply made knock-off to function like the real thing. She knew that first hand. After all, her homemade maid began to leave a syrupy slug-like trail through the house within weeks of reanimation. And she'd never been much good at cunnilingus or doing windows either.

Still, the political climate continued to decline from bad to worse, and soon became hard to ignore as it continued to worsen. When the government issued a recall of all commercial zombies, Lydia began to worry. Then they issued the order for National Guard troops to round up any help remaining in people's residences. That is when panic finally sat in.

Eventually, the day she dreaded came. The doorbell rang, and when Lydia opened her door, she found herself staring into the faces of two MP's.

"Good evening, Ma'am," the taller one greeted her.

"Yes? Can I help you?" Lydia asked, assuming her most submissive old woman persona.

The shorter one stepped forward brandishing a clipboard. "Our records indicate that you have a zombie house servant," he said.

"Oh, yes, I did, but she didn't work out so well. I had to bury her in the backyard," Lydia said.

The taller MP nodded, but his partner looked down at his clipboard and furrowed his brow. "But this says that you own a male zombie, Ma'am."

"What? Let me see that," Lydia said, frowning as she snatched the clipboard from him.

"Well, this is obviously a mistake," she said firmly.

"But, Ma'am..."

"No, this must be a computer error," she pronounced. "Your forms say 'M,' but they should say 'F.' Someone obviously checked the wrong box. I had a female zombie. She wasn't very good at her job, so when she started to go rancid, I just buried her in the garden. Take a look for yourself."

The two men whispered to each other briefly, then one went back to the truck. Soon, a team of serious-looking men in hazmat suits emerged and immediately set to work digging up Lydia's flower bed. It took them about an hour to unearth all the pieces of the maid, turn the earth thoroughly to make sure they hadn't missed any bits, and then cart all the refuse away.

After the work was done, the two MP's returned to her door.

"We just need you to sign off here, Ma'am," the shorter one said, proffering his clipboard.

Lydia signed, eager for them to leave. But he lingered in the doorway, leaning into her house suspiciously.

"Forgive me for saying so, Ma'am, but your house smells a bit... *ripe,*" he said.

"Well," Lydia snapped, straightening her house dress indignantly, "if I'd expected company, I would have washed."

"Oh, that's alright," he said, flustered. "I'm sorry Ma'am." He exchanged a glance with his partner.

"Well, if you two gentlemen are finished with your witch hunt, I'd like to get back to my supper," Lydia said.

"Of course," said the taller man. "We apologize for the inconvenience."

Lydia shut the door and let out a sigh of relief.

****

"She was substandard fertilizer anyway," Lydia quipped to Heracles after she had retrieved him from the air vent in which she had crammed him. Heracles, of course, said nothing.

Lydia pitied her neighbors, who all now lacked necro-help. How burdensome all those household tasks must be!

Thanks to her quick thinking, she need never worry about such things. She had retained her beloved illicit zombie, so her household would continue to be well-maintained. More importantly, she would remain sexually satisfied, maintaining her regimen of multiple daily orgasms.

"I always thought Daisy was a good for nothing," she mused. "But she sure turned out to be handy when all this fuss cropped up over civilians owning zombies. Yep, that good for nothing daughter of yours was finally good for something, after all," she pronounced, cradling Heracles' sunken face.

Nobody was going to take Heracles away from her now.

"They'll have to pry your cock out of my cold, dead hands," she cooed at him, fondling his prosthetic phallus.

Good Enough to Eat

As Lydia had grown older, time had taken its toll. Her skin had lost the last of its elasticity, and her ample bosom drooped, hanging pendulous when she released it from the confines of her bra.

What little vanity she had clung to in her forties and fifties was now gone, having been shed little by little, year by year. The final insult had come only recently, when Lydia had gotten dentures.

There is a point at which every aging woman must relinquish her fantasies about her own appearance, no longer able to pretend to have allure, even to herself. That moment had finally come for Lydia with the loss of her teeth. It's very difficult to make toothlessness seem sexy.

But Lydia was fortunate. She needn't worry about losing her lover along with the last of her looks. There was no need for her to feel self-conscious; her companion would never leave her. She would always be good enough for him. He had no will of his own.

There was a downside to the path she had chosen in life, of course. Having a zombie for a companion was limiting in several regards. For instance, Heracles wasn't much of a conversationalist. His most elaborate response to her prattling and commands came only in the form of guttural grunts. It was a lonely existence, but an emotionally safe one -- and, sexually, a consistently satisfying one. No matter how decrepit Lydia became, Heracles would still service her without complaint.

Still mostly asleep, Lydia twisted in the bed, shifting her cellulite-laden thighs and moaning softly with pleasure.

His head was between her legs; the scrappy remains of his hair tickled her inner thighs as he moved his face. Lydia tilted her pelvis up to give Heracles a better angle.

She loved waking up like this. There was no better way to be roused into consciousness than by having her muff eaten.

But something wasn't right. She had a nagging feeling. What was it?

Pain. Yes, pain. That's what it was. A sharp, nagging sensation of pain.

Lydia rubbed her eyes with one hand while trying to push Heracles' head away with the other, but he was performing cunnilingus with unusual tenacity this morning.

"Mmmm, stop, Heracles," she mumbled, trying to scoot herself away from his flicking tongue.

Her pussy felt so wet - far wetter than it had in years. Was he even using a dental dam?

"Heracles, stop," Lydia said more forcefully, now using both hands to try to push his mouth away from her throbbing vagina. He wouldn't budge, latched on like a leech to her, and her hands came away sticky.

Blood.

Why was she bleeding?

"Heracles!" she shouted, now suddenly fully awake. "Stop! Stop!"

Instead of heeding her commands, Heracles only munched down on her with renewed enthusiasm. In fact, it was the only time she had ever seen Heracles express enthusiasm. He was actually smiling, sporting a Cheshire cat-like toothy grin between each bite.

Toothy? Her dentures! Looking around frantically, she suddenly realized that her dentures weren't on her bedside table.

"No!" Lydia shrieked as the zombie ate her snatch.

With her dentures, caked with blood and pubic hair, sitting firmly in his mouth, Heracles finished devouring her pelvic region and, as she thrashed beneath him, he pulled himself up to her breasts, tearing strips of stretch-marked flesh from them with a voracious appetite.

When Lydia was younger, she might have been strong enough to fight him off, but she had become old and weak. All she could do was cry pleadingly for him to stop and ineffectually strike at his back as he ate her.

And ate he did.

Tearful, Lydia croaked her final words in disbelief, "You weren't happy together?" Then Heracles unburdened her of her throat.

All the while, his pelvic region gently gyrated, as if the repetitive task had become so ingrained that his body now performed it reflexively. In fact, after she had long since expired, Heracles still ground his hips against her pieces as he gorged himself, as if still seeking to satisfy his mistress as he consumed her.

When Heracles was done, the bed was soaked in blood and dotted with shreds of flesh. This, and her skeletal frame, were all that remained of Lydia.

Clumsily pulling bits of his mistress from the dentures, his newest prosthetic accessory, Heracles' face cracked in several places as he drew his mouth into a broad smile. Although capable of only very limited thought or sensation, he knew that he felt whole for the first time in ages.

His day had finally come.

Undead, but Not Forgotten

He was only spoken of in hushed whispers - perhaps he didn't really exist at all. An urban legend passed in clandestine conversations between discontented housewives. Surely no such zombie really existed - a perfect organic sex machine, its skills in producing sexual gratification honed to fine precision.

So, when Sarah saw him, she was sure she had been misled. This couldn't be the mythical zombie sex king. In fact, this was hardly even a zombie. It was so old and rotten that most of it had been replaced with prosthesis or cybernetic parts. And the way it was being kept – shoved in the back corner of an old van, tied unceremoniously to a dilapidated old gurney for so long that bits of the torn thin foam padding had begun to mingle and fuse with the zombie's glistening decomposed flesh – was hardly fitting of a sexual legend.

This was no god. This was just a sad, festering corpse.

Though disappointed, Sarah was not surprised. Zombies had been illegalized decades ago, after a rash of incidents involving improperly zombified husbands. Rendered zombies by undersexed spouses who failed to adequately de-teeth or preserve them, they had rapidly become a public health hazard. Not to mention that quite a few wound up eating their families.

After that, the government had taken all the zombies away - presumably to destroy them.

Occasionally, one still popped up here or there, but they were unskilled, spastic things - just pathetic echoes of the former working dead - nothing more than uncoordinated, stumbling buckets of putrid flesh.

Still, she was here, and she had paid a lot of money, so she felt compelled to give this zombie a closer look.

She approached gingerly, watching as it worked its jaws, gnashing fetid gums with increasing fervor as she drew nearer.

The blackened, desiccated skin of its face was stretched impossibly taut, leaving nothing about its skull's bone structure to the imagination, and it wore a dirty, tattered apron that was rife with stains.

The apron's a nice tough, Sarah thought.

Its lifeless cybernetic arm dangled loosely from its shoulder joint, frayed wiring peeking out from where it was separating.

She was surprised that they had paid such attention to detail. Why take such trouble only to shove it in the back of a van?

Then she noticed that it was gyrating its hips suggestively.

What the hell?

Tentatively lifting one corner of its befouled apron, Sarah found herself gazing down at a massive prosthetic penis, standing rigid in a festering organic socket.

"Oh, my God!" she breathed. "You *are* Heracles!"

*****

Sarah climbed atop his gurney, straddling him, and stretched to reach the metal pulley that hung above his head. The black leather straps of the harness they had given her to wear, which intersected in an x across her chest and ran tightly under her breasts, bit into her skin as she strained to clip the end of her chain into the pulley above the bed.

He was already strapped in, of course. Coarse leather straps kept him restrained and also prevented him from falling off of the gurney while the van was in motion; the jostling motion of the vehicle could be quite violent.

Once Sarah's line was secure, she lowered herself down next to him. His organic arm, still mostly functional, was welcoming, embracing her.

Ravenous for him, she wrapped herself around him, burying herself in his bare neck. She licked his grey flesh, nibbling deliriously, sucking, drawing her tongue across that intoxicating expanse of exposed, flaking flesh. Sarah lapped at it, consuming his detritus as if it were the most delicious thing she had ever tasted.

Heracles had been Sarah's fantasy for so many years now. She didn't care about infection, about anything after this. She just gave herself to this moment.

Playfully, lovingly, she fingered his eye sockets, mimicking the motion and rhythm she knew that he would soon adopt inside of her.

Then a wave of panic gripped her. She had paid for half an hour. It was all Sarah had really been able to afford, and she had been so sure that it would turn out to be another hoax. How much time did she have left?

She had been leading up to riding him, building her arousal to a fever-pitch, but Sarah had made a mistake in taking her time; the convoy lurched to a stop, almost throwing her from his raised cot, and effectively cutting short their interlude together.

"Time's up!" a gruff voice shouted from outside the van, rapping on its side.

Stealing a final kiss, a quick flick of the tongue between his dry, mummified parted lips, Sarah paused for one brief moment to look down at him wistfully. His sunken face was more gorgeous to her than the chiseled features or creamy, smooth skin of any live man could

69

ever be. Heracles, for her, was a goddamned rock star, the epitome of all of her long-lost school girl fantasies. Except, of course, as a school girl, she had yearned for love, for romance, for commitment -- for "forever." It's funny how time and hormones change a woman. As she had grown older, and her needs had changed, she had become more and more fixated upon this zombie prince, this king of sexual service. She just wanted to devour him, to wreck him, to use him up -- to tear that withered body apart, savoring each mouthful, cracking him wide open and sucking the marrow from his lovely bones when she was done.

It was with deep regret that Sarah hurriedly unhooked her chain and rushed out to return to the lackluster world outside.

About the Author

Alisha Adkins is the author of the zombie novellas *Flesh Eaters, Making the Best of the Zombie Apocalypse,* and *Zombie Gras* and other works of horror and speculative fiction.
She is a native of New Orleans, where she lives with her husband, dog, and cat. Alisha Adkins holds a Masters degree from the University of New Orleans, and has worked as a teacher, consultant, eBay Powerseller, webmaster, and forum moderator. She is currently pursuing her dream of writing and quietly starving to death.

Excerpt from Making the Best of the Zombie Apocalypse

Chapter 1 - Keeping Mother

I have kept my mother chained to the frame of her bed for a little over two years now. I don't even really hear the racket she makes anymore. The scraping of her chains against the metal frame, her moaning, and the spluttering, guttural noises -- they're all just background sounds now, as natural as the chirping of birds or the hum of crickets.

How long should we hold onto our zombie children or zombie mothers out of sentimentality, a sense of duty, or unwillingness to accept change? Behavioral scientists could undoubtedly make good research of this question, if they weren't all busy studying zombies or being zombies themselves these days.

I know it's not my mother anymore. It's just the flesh that my mother used to inhabit. Soulless, hungry flesh. To be honest, it doesn't really even look much like my mother anymore.

And I know that keeping her can only serve to do me harm -- living with a corpse inevitably produces unhygienic living conditions and promotes an unhealthy mental state. On top of that, there is a certain level of stress that is unavoidable when you live with the knowledge that something that wants to eat you is never more than a room or two away. And that's not to mention the very real and ever present danger that she may eventually succeed...

Still, letting her go is unthinkable.

I mean, what can I do? She's my mother.

****

After my divorce, I moved in with my mother. She was getting on in years, and I was worried about her being all alone in her house in the suburbs. I did it for her sake, but her companionship helped ease my own loneliness as well. I'd gone from living in a house teeming with life -- a wife, two young children and a dog

-- to living in a chillingly silent, unnaturally still apartment literally overnight. My wife had full custody, and I found myself working longer and longer hours just so I didn't have to face the emptiness of my new "home." So, if I'm really honest with myself, moving in with Mother benefited us both. Even if she was just puttering around in another room, I found the sounds of her presence comforting. In some ways, I guess I still do.

Mother and I lived together about three years before the End of Days, as my mother called it, and about another year after the zombies came. "Nathan," she used to say -- my name is Nathan, by the way -- "Nathan, it's the end time now. Judgment Day is upon us." She never quite worked out why judgment never came or, if it had, why *everyone* had apparently been condemned to suffer.

Now I still live with Mother, but she no longer lives at all.

Some days, I don't even go into her room. It's easier when I don't have to look at her. On those days, I can just go about my daily routine. Everything is normal, and the scratching, rustling, and moaning are just vague reminders of having some companionship within the house. I tell myself that Mother is just a little sick right now, that's all.

Zombies don't actually get colds, of course, though I did once think that Mother must be coming down with the sniffles when her nose started to run. It turned out to just be her brain liquefying.

Sometimes I feel as though I'm a terrible son. I mean, I keep my mother chained by her hands and feet to the bed. And I don't really feed her. Under the circumstances, I think I've done the best I could, but it still certainly sounds callous if you put it down in words.

Other than a few rats that I've trapped, Mother hasn't eaten in two years. So, I'm sure that Mother is extremely hungry. The problem is that she won't eat anything that isn't alive. When I first restrained her in her bedroom and began my "hospice" care, I tried to feed her soup. That was a disaster. Then, for my next attempt at feeding her, I tried giving her scraps of humans and animals that I had scavenged, but she still showed not even the faintest interest. Flesh is apparently uninteresting to her if it doesn't still retain the warmth of life. The only meal she consistently expresses desire for is me.

Today, I knew I had to tidy up in her room. I'd put it off for far too long.

As soon as I open the door, the heavy wave of stench hits me.

One step back, deliberately exhale, and then, back rigid, I enter. I have ritualized this task by now. Somehow, it makes it easier.

One quick burst of Lysol to try to dilute the air. I'd like to spray more, but it has to be conserved.

Flies buzz against the windows. If Mother could reach them, perhaps they would provide a snack. I swat them with a rolled up newspaper. The sheer, once yellow, curtains are tattered and stained. I brush off the crushed flies that have adhered to the fabric. I'll sweep them up before I leave.

Using a bucket and sponge, I attempt (rather futilely) to remove the gunk and splatters that have most recently accumulated upon the walls. This is my routine.

Once I have run out of other tasks in the room, I finally turn to Mother.

She is straining against her chains, leaning as far forward on the bed as the shackles will allow.

Though it was at great personal risk to myself, I used to try to wipe down my mother. After all, in order to respect her memory, I felt that her body deserved to be maintained with some level of dignity. However, after I realized that the rag I used to wipe off her ooze and muck was also coming away with skin and the occasional bone fragment, I gave up on the practice.

So, if I allow myself to be honest about it, Mother looks pretty damned bad.

I try not to examine her features, but some things I still can't avoid noticing. Lately, I've begun to think that her jaw is coming loose. Not that there is anything I can do about that.

Mother wears an old house dress. If I remember correctly, it used to be blue. It's hardly more than a filth-soaked rag now that loosely drapes her withered frame. I would try to change her clothes, but there is just no way to adequately subdue her.

My mother has worn that dress since the day she passed. I guess, in some small way, I have a grown a sentimental attachment to it over the years.

****

Unfortunately, after she was bitten, Mother did not die right away.

After the End Time began, I saw that my mother never left the safety of the house. I took care of all of the supply gathering and our other needs. She was in her sixties, after all. I was the good, dutiful, protective son I should have been. I continue to remind myself of this, to console myself with this.

Mother was infected by a young woman that she innocently let into our home. While I was away on a supply run, a woman of about twenty had come to our door. She made a great deal of noise, pleading to be let in.

"I heard someone moving around in there. And I saw light from your window. Please, I know there's

79

someone alive in there. There are zombies out here --
I'm scared. Please, please let me in!"

Mother was a softy. She let the girl in, fed her,
and comforted her, listening to the girl's story. One thing
about End Time -- everyone has a story to tell.

I think Mother thought that I needed a girlfriend.
But she didn't realize that this girl could not make a
suitable mate. She had been bitten, though she
concealed it from both of us.

When I returned home that evening, I was
exasperated with Mother for letting her inside our house.
The girl could have been part of a group that was laying
in wait out of sight to swarm our residence and claim it
for themselves. Anything could have happened, really. I
privately scolded her for not being careful enough.

"Please be more careful, Mother! You're all I
have. What if something happened to you? Please don't
put yourself in danger."

My mother had just smiled and patted my arm.

It did seem like we'd dodged a bullet, though.
The girl was nice, and kind of cute besides. We ate
dinner together (some cans of beans I had found in an

abandoned house earlier that day), chatted affably, and then Mother put out pillows and a quilt for the girl to sleep on our sofa.

The girl died quietly while lying on our sofa that night. She returned less quietly -- Mother, always a light sleeper, heard her knocking about and bumping into things -- and went to see what was happening (she was probably worried that one of her collection of glass figurines would be broken in the ruckus).

The girl -- or former girl, or whatever I should call her -- attacked my mother, taking a hefty bite out of her forearm before I was able to run into the living room and peel her off of my mother.

I smashed that bitch corpse's skull in with one of Mother's heavier crystal figurines -- a blue jay, I think it was -- that still sat intact upon the end table. I kept hitting until there was just a pile of muck where her head should have been.

But why do I play this over yet again in my mind? It's old news, and nothing can be changed now. After being bitten, Mother suffered through terrible pain for several days before she succumbed to the infection and died. I had the foresight to restrain her. Now we live together in a different way.

There's something horrifying about the notion of seeing something you love corrupted and defiled. But, if you see it often enough, you get used to it. It becomes the new normal. As upsetting as it is to live with the zombified remains of my mother, I can't imagine how I'd fill my days now without her... Looking after Mother, and keeping our environment relatively sanitary in spite of her, gives me purpose and provides a daily routine. And, as tragic as it may be, when I look into the vacant sockets that once contained her eyes, memories of my boyhood still flood back to me.

Sitting slightly forward and staring blankly into the depths of those sockets as I sat next to Mother's bed in the bergére chair that she had so lovingly and painstakingly reupholstered nearly a decade ago, when my ex-wife, Becky, was pregnant with our first child, I guess that I got lost in my thoughts. Before I realized what was happening, Mother lunged for me, grazing my cheek with her desiccated lips. A millimeter closer and her teeth would have made contact before I was able to draw back.

I gasped as I pulled back from her with such sudden force that I practically tipped my chair over backwards. Adrenaline rushing and heart pounding in my ears, I unconsciously pushed the chair away with my long legs, finding myself already a good three feet away before I was even conscious of what I was doing.

My zombie mother's head was still thrust forward, matted clumps of her unkempt hair falling over her face, mercifully obscuring her misshapen features, although I could still make out her teeth fiercely gnashing.

I sat very still and let my heart slowly return to its normal pace.

She -- it -- was still occasionally jerking against her chains, though I think she sensed that her opportunity had passed. Her motions lacked their previous fervor, as though she had resigned herself to the fact that, at least for the time being, her efforts were destined to be fruitless.

After about five minutes, I was breathing normally and my heart had grown quiet again. I looked at the book on the end table which now sat between the bed and the chair in which I sat. It was a book I had read many times. Unfortunately, I had left most of my library in storage after my divorce, and Mother's collection had been limited, especially once you sifted out the books on needlepoint and positive affirmations. Since I was essentially a shut-in by necessity, and there was no electricity for television or Internet, reading at the window was my primary diversion. I generally liked to spend a few hours reading at Mother's bedside, just for the company our presences might afford one another. Today, since Mother had almost eaten me, I decided to forgo it.

Letting out a sigh, I got up, returned the chair to its standard position in the room, mumbled my usual goodbye to Mother with less conviction than usual, and left the room, locking the door behind me.

Excerpt from Death: the Travelogues

Prologue

The nice thing about death is that it makes all of your problems inconsequential. However, this is primarily because, typically, death means the end of consciousness, and all of the needling little inconveniences that come along with it – obligations, embarrassments, worries over trivial matters...

I seem to have been part of some tiny cosmic glitch – a miniscule hole in the fabric of existence, or maybe a just a hiccup, one random number out of place in the gigantic computer program of life.

I died, but my consciousness failed to turn off. This was rather unpleasant until I figured out that I didn't need my physical body. Being a consciousness trapped in a rotting husk of meat is rather disconcerting. The living are so accustomed to the organic transports that carry them around that they often cannot separate their concepts of self from their own bodies. I was guilty of similar ignorance. It did not occur to me that my body and I were no longer tethered together. I languished in my own putrid, wrecked remains for well over a week before I figured out that I could just get out and walk.

I imagine that you are wondering then, do I have no physical form? Well, yes, and no. Bodies are merely vehicles for transporting people's consciousnesses around. So, I occasionally hitch a ride.

"Possession" is an ugly word; it is laden with negative associations. There is no malice inherent in what I do; I'm just catching a lift. Sometimes I sit in the back seat and enjoy the scenery. Sometimes I drive.

To brazenly mix metaphors, imagine that you ate the same meal every day of your life. Maybe it is a good meal, or maybe it is an unpalatable one. Regardless, it is always the same one. If you suddenly had a chance to try every conceivable dish currently prepared on the planet, wouldn't you jump at the chance? Well, I would.

A single life is myopic; only since death, with a smorgasbord of bodies available to inhabit, have I begun to form a vague conception of human existence.

Bodies are so… limiting. Being confined to one body, imprisoned in a single ambulatory shell, is so depressingly narrow an existence that it makes me feel claustrophobic to even contemplate it. I can't fathom how I ever was able to stand it. No wonder I was unhappy; no wonder, essentially, at least deep down, all living people are.

I want it to be clear that I am not a ghost or a spirit. If my spirit did survive death, I'm sure it's contentedly floating around a forest somewhere, suffusing with nature. Whatever it is doing, if it exists, has nothing to do with me. I was once a person, but now I am merely a consciousness, or simply an entity. What I was in life doesn't matter; I was the sum of my limited experiences. But, still, my aim is not to be unsettling, and the living tend to find comfort in familiarity, so I suppose I should make an attempt to have you "get to know me." I'll start from the beginning.

www.ingramcontent.com/pod-product-compliance
Lightning Source LLC
Chambersburg PA
CBHW071342130626
46556CB00005B/1983